THE CREEPER ATTACK

THE CREEPER ATTACK

AN UNOFFICIAL MINECRAFTERS TIME TRAVEL ADVENTURE

BOOK TWO

Winter Morgan

Sky Pony Press
New York

Copyright © 2018 by Hollan Publishing, Inc.

Minecraft® is a registered trademark of Notch Development AB.

The Minecraft game is copyright © Mojang AB.

Sky Pony Press books may be purchased in bulk at special discounts for sales promotion, corporate gifts, fund-raising, or educational purposes. Special editions can also be created to specifications. For details, contact the Special Sales Department, Sky Pony Press, 307 West 36th Street, 11th Floor, New York, NY 10018 or info@skyhorsepublishing.com.

Sky Pony® is a registered trademark of Skyhorse Publishing, Inc.®, a Delaware corporation.

Minecraft® is a registered trademark of Notch Development AB.
The Minecraft game is copyright © Mojang AB.

Visit our website at www.skyponypress.com.

10 9 8 7 6 5 4 3 2 1

Library of Congress Cataloging-in-Publication Data is available on file.

Cover design by Brian Peterson
Cover photo by Megan Miller

Print ISBN: 978-1-5107-3736-5
Ebook ISBN: 978-1-5107-3741-9

Printed in Canada

TABLE OF CONTENTS

THE CREEPER ATTACK

1

THE INVITATION

"I have big news." Brett and Joe stood in the entrance to Poppy's house. They were breathless because they had sprinted all the way to her door. Both of them were eager to tell Poppy their good news.

Poppy smiled. "I have something to tell you, too!"

Brett blurted out, "Really? That's great. We can't wait to hear. Tell us."

"No, you first," said Poppy.

"We're going to the cold taiga to build a farm," Brett exclaimed.

"That's amazing, and it also makes my news even better," said Poppy.

"What's your news?" asked Joe.

"I am going to the taiga to build a large igloo and a castle. I was commissioned by the town to build those two buildings." Poppy asked, "When do you guys have to go to the taiga? I have to leave tomorrow."

"So do we," said Brett.

"This is great. Let's craft an igloo, and then we can be roommates," suggested Poppy.

"Sounds like a plan," Brett said.

Poppy looked up at the sky. It was getting dark, and she caught a glance of two vacant-eyed zombies lumbering toward her house. "Oh no! Zombies! You guys have to head home. It's not safe out."

"Where?" Joe pulled armor and a diamond sword from his inventory, caught sight of the zombies, and raced toward them.

Brett put on his armor and joined Joe in the battle against the undead beasts that spawned when the sun began to set. They slammed their swords into the zombies, piercing the oozing flesh and weakening the creatures until they were destroyed. Brett and Joe leaned down to pick up the rotten flesh from the ground, but both let out a collective gasp when they spotted an army of zombies marching into the town.

"I can help!" Poppy rushed toward them dressed in armor. She fearlessly lunged at the smelly beasts, trying to destroy as many as she could. Brett splashed potions on the zombies while Joe ripped into the creatures with his diamond sword. Poppy was down to one heart when the final zombie was destroyed.

"Take this." Joe handed her a potion to restore her energy.

Poppy sipped the potion as she checked out the area for any other hostile mobs that spawned in the dark. "I think we're safe," she said. "You guys should stay at my house tonight. It's not safe for you to travel home."

Brett and Joe followed Poppy back to her house. As they reached her door, Brett felt a stinging pain radiate down his arm.

"A spider jockey!" screamed Joe.

Poppy put away her sword and grabbed a bow and arrow, and with perfect aim, she struck the skeleton that rode atop the red-eyed spider. Her second arrow destroyed the bony beast. Brett ripped into the spider while Poppy picked up the dropped bones on the grass. It took three precise hits from Brett's sword, but he destroyed the deadly arachnoid.

"We have to get inside," Poppy said.

The gang hurried into the house and closed the door. "We need to get up early," said Brett. "We should get to sleep."

Poppy led them to the extra bedroom. Joe thanked Poppy for letting them stay at her house. Joe and Brett wearily climbed into their beds. Brett pulled the wool blanket over his tired body. As he drifted off to sleep, he thought about the challenges of building a farm in the ice biome. He needed to figure out a way to melt the snow. When he realized the best method was using a torch, he scanned his inventory for torches, but he had only a couple in his inventory.

"We need torches," he called out, but Joe was already fast asleep. Brett could hear him snoring.

Brett tossed and turned and couldn't fall asleep. He was anxious about the trip to the taiga. He didn't want to show up unprepared, but they weren't given a lot of time to prepare for the journey. Brett wondered why all of them were invited to the taiga at the same time. He started to think these offers might be slightly suspicious, but then he told himself that he was just overtired and his mind was wandering. Brett focused on the beauty of the taiga and the snowmen he would build during his time off. He rarely traveled outside of Meadow Mews, and he wanted to be excited for this opportunity rather than suspicious of the town's people and their motives for inviting this trio.

Brett didn't even remember falling asleep. He awoke and looked over at Joe, but his friend was missing.

"Joe," Brett called out, but there was no response.

He jumped out of the bed as he heard Poppy's ocelot meow. "Sam," Brett said to the ocelot, "where is everyone?" He knew asking the ocelot was pointless; the small animal couldn't speak. The ocelot stared at him, meowed, and rubbed against his legs, leading Brett to assume the animal was hungry. He pulled some fish from his inventory and fed Poppy's pet while he called out for his two friends. "Poppy! Joe!"

"Brett," Poppy raced into the house, "we were just filling our inventories with apples and other treats from the farm."

Joe handed Brett a bunch of apples. "This is for you."

"Thanks," said Brett as he placed the apples in his inventory.

"Well, now that we have food," said Poppy, "we

should get going. The trip to the taiga takes about a day, and I don't want us to get stuck outside at night."

"Good idea," said Joe as he looked through his inventory, making sure he had all the supplies he planned to bring with him.

"There's just one problem: we need torches to melt the snow, or we won't be able to farm. Do you have any torches, Joe?" asked Brett.

"I have three," he replied after searching through his inventory.

"We're going to need more than that," explained Brett. "We won't be able to find coal in that biome. We must mine on the way there so we have enough coal to craft torches when we need them. I have a bunch of sticks in my inventory, so we don't need to get those."

Poppy studied the map. "No problem, there's a mountain biome on the way there. If we make a quick trip to a cave, we can find a bunch of coal. I'll help you get some."

The gang looked through their inventories as they set off on their one-day journey to the cold biome.

As they walked through the meadow and into the forest, Poppy said, "Do you find anything strange about the timing of these invitations?"

"What do you mean?" asked Joe.

Brett asked, "Do you think it's strange because we were all asked to go to the taiga and we weren't given a lot of advance notice?"

"Yes," said Poppy. "That's exactly what I was thinking."

"You guys only think that way because you're both pranksters and you always believe someone is going to trick you. I don't think there is anything strange about the invitation," said Joe.

"Then why do you think they asked us to come right away, Joe?" Poppy questioned.

"Perhaps somebody canceled," suggested Joe.

"Makes sense," Brett said with a chuckle. "Maybe Joe's right. We just always think everyone wants to trick us because *we* always trick people."

"It's been awhile since we've tricked anyone," Poppy said. "We should plan a good prank soon."

"You better not pull a prank on me," said Joe.

"Let's plan a prank on the folks in the taiga," suggested Poppy.

"What would you do?" asked Joe.

Poppy giggled. "I don't know. But we have an advantage there because nobody knows us, and they aren't expecting to be tricked."

Joe reminded Poppy, "You guys have a reputation. I had heard about your pranking before I came to Meadow Mews. You've pulled off some pretty large-scale pranks. I think you guys should stop pranking people. It's not very nice."

"Oh come on. We only do it to be funny," Poppy defended them. "Right, Brett?"

Brett wasn't paying attention to their conversation. He was too fixated on the fact that they were all invited to the taiga. Although he was glad to be with Poppy, the more he thought about it, the more he felt there was something unsettling about the invitation. As the trio walked deeper into the forest, Brett stayed close to his friends because he didn't want to get lost in the thick leaves. He hoped Joe was right and that he was invited to the taiga simply because they wanted him to build a farm and that nothing sinister was in the works.

2

CREATURES OF THE SWAMP

Poppy paused and pulled out the map. "I think we're lost," she said as she stared at the swamp biome in the distance. "I don't see the swamp biome on this map."

Brett and Joe leaned over Poppy to see the map. "You're right," said Brett. "There isn't a swamp on the map. Who gave you this map?"

"They sent it with the invitation," replied Poppy.

"That's strange," said Brett. "We didn't receive a map with our invitation."

"Really?" Poppy looked at the map again. "Look at this. We are supposed to be in the jungle. I have no idea why we're by the swamp."

A thunderous boom shook the Overworld. As rain fell from the sky, it made noise when it fell against the lush green leaves of the trees. Brett said, "We should stay here. I don't think it's a good idea to be in the swamp during the rainstorm. There are enough hostile mobs that are able to spawn here, and we don't want to have to battle the ones that are spawning in the swamp, too."

"Ouch!" Poppy screamed as an arrow hit her back. She turned around to find two skeletons standing in her path.

She lunged toward the bony beasts with her diamond sword, ripping into the skeletons and instantly destroying one. She struck the second skeleton. As its bones clanged, she saw an arrow strike the beast and obliterate it. Poppy turned around and saw Brett aiming his bow and arrow. He called out, "Have you seen Joe?"

"No," said Poppy as the rain drenched her hair and raindrops ran down her face, clouding her vision.

"Joe!" Brett hollered, but there was no response. He couldn't find his friend.

"He couldn't have gone very far." Poppy looked around, trying to catch sight of Joe in the dense forest.

"Maybe he went to the swamp," suggested Brett.

"Or maybe he was destroyed and respawned in Meadow Mews," Poppy said. She didn't want to search through the swamp in a rainstorm. She didn't want to look for trouble.

"He could have respawned in Meadow Mews, but I think it's more likely that he ran from a hostile mob and made his way into the swamp."

"I don't think we should venture into the swamp. You know how I get around witches." Poppy shuddered. "And slimes."

Brett knew Poppy disliked the swamp and tried to avoid it at all costs, but today they had to go. They had to find Joe.

"Brett! Poppy!" Joe called out, but they couldn't see him.

"Where are you?" screamed Brett.

"Help!" Joe hollered.

"We don't know where you are!" Poppy called out as she looked for Joe in the trees but didn't see him.

"A witch!" Joe cried.

"I knew it," Brett said. "He's in the swamp. We have to go."

Poppy's heart felt like it was pounding out of her body as she followed behind Brett and into the rainy swamp biome. Before they could see Joe, Poppy heard a familiar noise that made her cringe.

Boing! Boing! Boing!

"Oh no," Poppy cried as three slimes surrounded them.

Brett pulled out his diamond sword and struck one of the slimes, which broke into smaller cubes. Poppy stood frozen in terror as she heard a shrill laugh from a witch.

"I think Joe is over there." She pointed to the direction where she had heard the witch's laughter.

"Help me!" Brett was irritated. "You need to destroy some of these slimes. I can't do it on my own."

Poppy took a deep breath as she ripped into the slimy creatures and then struck the smaller slimes. When the final slime was destroyed, the rain stopped.

"Thankfully, the rain is over," Poppy said with relief.

Joe raced toward his friends. "The witch. I destroyed the witch," he said between sips at a bottle of milk, which he offered to his friends.

Poppy declared, "I want to get out of the swamp right now. I don't want to spend any time here."

"I agree," said Brett, "but let's look at the map."

Poppy took out the map. "This is useless. It doesn't have the swamp on it at all. I have no idea how to get to the cold biome."

Joe said, "I actually went to the biome before, and I think I have an idea of how to get there. We should rush through the rest of the swamp, and then we should be in the mountainous biome."

"We must stop in that biome. Don't forget that we have to mine for coal or we won't be able to melt the ice," said Brett.

"Of course I didn't forget," said Joe.

The gang bolted through the swamp biome. As they got deeper into the swampy biome, the group collectively hoped that the mountainous biome was close, but it seemed as if they were in the swamp a lot longer than they had expected. Poppy looked up at the sky.

"Guys," her voice cracked, "I see a full moon."

"We have to pick up the speed," Brett said as two bats flew past them.

"I think it's too late," Joe hollered as a witch clutching a vial of potion hurtled toward him. The witch splashed it on Joe, and he couldn't move. His body was exhausted.

Poppy stared at the witch. She had to overcome her fear of this purple-robed monster. If she didn't lunge at the witch alongside Brett, they might be trapped in the swamp.

With a renewed energy, Poppy slammed her sword deep into the witch's belly. The witch was able to sprinkle a few drops of potion on Poppy, weakening her. Poppy had enough energy to grab a potion from her inventory to help her regain strength as she watched Brett destroy the witch.

"Take this." Brett raced to Joe, handing him a potion to regain his strength. Joe drank it.

The sun was beginning to set, and Poppy said, "We have to keep moving. We can't get stuck here."

The trio jogged alongside the murky swamp water and didn't stop until they saw the peak of a mountain.

"It's the mountainous biome," Poppy called out gleefully.

"We have to find shelter," said Joe as he saw two skeletons racing toward them. The skeletons shot arrows as the gang rushed with their swords and attacked the beasts. As they picked up the dropped bones, Poppy said, "Look! There's an opening to a cave."

Brett followed Poppy into the cave. He hoped nobody was hiding in it, waiting to attack them.

3

MADNESS IN THE MINE

The first thing they saw in the cave was a pair of red eyes staring at them. Brett raced over to the cave spider and slammed his sword into the creepy eight-legged creature.

Poppy jumped back as she pointed toward the ground. "Look at the silverfish."

The ground was covered in silverfish bugs. They hit the bugs, obliterating the insects that blanketed the cave's dirt floor.

When they had destroyed the final silverfish, Brett said, "We have to start mining for coal."

"Don't you think we should get some sleep?" asked Joe with a yawn.

"Not now. We're in the cave. This is the time we should get some coal. If we don't have coal, we shouldn't even bother heading to the cold biome," Brett said as he banged his pickaxe into the ground. But he didn't see any coal.

"Maybe we shouldn't go to the cold biome," suggested Joe. This was the first time he started to believe there might be trouble in the cold biome. Why was the map wrong? He had been attacked in the swamp, and he wondered if his friends were right about their being set up. "Maybe you guys were right and we will be tricked. Look at what happened with the map. I just think that's a bad sign."

"We might be," said Brett, "but we made a commitment to the people of the taiga." Brett banged his pickaxe again. As he reached another layer of blocks, he spotted a piece of coal. "I found coal!" he called out.

Poppy hurried toward Brett's side and hit her pickaxe against the ground. She found another piece of coal. "It looks like we found a patch that has a lot of coal, and it seems like we're lucky."

Brett pulled coal from the hole they had dug. "If we keep finding coal, we will be able to get some sleep tonight."

Joe wasn't helping them unearth the coal. He was pacing the length of the cave, saying, "I have a feeling we shouldn't go to the cold biome."

"Can we stop talking about this?" Brett was annoyed. He wanted Joe to help him pull coal from the mine. "I want to go to the cold biome and start a farm. It's a challenge I've always wanted to take, and I never had the opportunity before to do something this big."

When Joe heard Brett speak, he remembered that

he also wanted to create a farm in an icy biome. It was a lifelong dream of his, and he decided that he would join Brett and Poppy and gather coal. Even though he worried they might be tricked while they were in the taiga, he knew it was a chance they had to take.

As they finished gathering coal and got ready to craft beds, they heard voices entering the cave.

"Who is there?" asked Brett as he pulled his diamond sword from his inventory.

Two people dressed in red jumpsuits walked inside the cave. They put their hands up. "Please, we aren't here to attack anyone. We are just looking for shelter," said the blue-haired girl in the red jumpsuit. "My name is Callie, and this is my friend Laura."

Her friend, dressed in the same outfit and sporting short black hair, added, "And we are looking for coal."

"Why are you here?" asked Poppy. She clutched her sword. She wasn't ready to trust these two people.

Laura said, "We're builders, and we were invited to build an ice castle in the taiga."

Poppy was shocked. "But I was asked to build an ice castle and an igloo."

"We weren't asked to build an igloo, but maybe they want to have more than one ice castle," said Callie.

"Did they give you a map?" asked Poppy.

"Yes," said Callie, "but it doesn't work. I mean, we tried using it, but it led us in the wrong direction."

"That's how we ended up in here. We just barely survived being in the swamp," said Laura. "And I hate the swamp. I have a fear of witches."

"So do I," said Poppy, and she introduced herself.

"Wow," said Callie, "you're Poppy? You're famous."

Laura added, "I can't believe we're actually meeting Poppy. Everyone in the Overworld knows about you."

Poppy blushed. "I am just a builder like you guys."

"I think we were probably hired to help you," said Callie. "We aren't well-known builders."

"Truthfully," Laura said, "we must confess that we were shocked that we were invited to the cold biome to help them build anything. We just built a tree house in our town and it has gotten some attention, but that's the first thing we ever built."

"That's strange," said Poppy, "but I assume your tree house was amazing. I'd love to see a picture of it. I've never built a tree house, but I've always wanted to build one."

Joe listened to Poppy, Callie, and Laura speak, and he began to grow even more suspicious of the invitation to the cold biome. He asked the group, "Don't you think it's odd that we are all invited to the taiga?"

Poppy said, "I think we should all head to the biome together. If this is a setup or a trap, we will stick together and get out of there."

"Poppy," Callie smiled, "aren't you known as a great prankster?"

"Yes," said Laura. "Everyone in the Overworld talks about how you pull pranks with your friend Brett."

Brett said, "We used to pull pranks. We don't do it much anymore."

"You're Brett?" asked Callie. "You're also famous."

Like Poppy, Brett also blushed. "I am just a farmer."

"You guys are so modest," said Callie, "but I'm so excited to meet both of you and work in the taiga with you."

Poppy offered to help the two young builders search for coal and then craft beds. "We should get some sleep before tomorrow."

The gang jumped back into the hole and mined for more coal. As they pulled pieces of coal from the ground, they tried to contain their yawning. They were all exhausted. When they finally had enough coal, the group checked the ground for silverfish and spiders, then crafted beds on the dirt floor.

Brett didn't have a hard time falling asleep. He was so tired from all of their adventures, and their job hadn't even begun. He hoped they'd find their way to the taiga the next morning. As he closed his eyes, he dreamed of farming in the taiga. He wanted to suggest to their new friends that they all share a large igloo in the taiga, but he looked over and realized he was the only one who was still awake.

Brett closed his eyes again, and when he awoke in the morning, he was shocked to see a familiar face standing above him.

4
ICE CASTLES

"**N**ancy?" Brett was surprised to see his friend from Meadow Mews.

"Brett?" she questioned as she spotted him. "Joe? Poppy? What are you guys doing here?"

"We can ask you the same question," said Brett.

"I'm on a treasure hunt," Nancy replied. "I told you guys I was going on a massive hunt, and when I spotted this cave, I thought I could mine for some minerals. I thought you guys were going to the taiga."

"We were." Brett stood up. "But the map led us in the wrong direction."

"That's strange," said Nancy. "Maps are usually accurate."

Callie and Laura walked over to them and introduced themselves. Callie mentioned that their map had also led them to the same cave. Nancy processed this information and said, "You know what's weird? I ran into a few people in the swamp who were also lost. They were standing there reading a map and asked me if I knew the correct way to the cold biome."

"I guess they need a lot of people for the project and they accidentally gave everyone the wrong map," said Brett. He wanted to rationalize the situation. He could see the sun shining through the narrow opening of the cave and said, "We have to get going to the cold biome now. Good luck on your treasure hunt, Nancy."

It was nice to see a familiar face in the middle of a journey. Nancy climbed into the hole and began to mine as they hurried out of the cave. Brett stared at the mountain in front of them, gasped, and asked, "We have to climb that mountain?"

"Yes," Joe said. "I think once we get to the other side, we should see the taiga."

"You think?" asked Brett. "I mean, what if we climb over the mountain and there isn't a taiga on the other side?"

"I've been to the taiga before, and we had to climb over this mountain. I'm almost a hundred percent sure that we will see it," said Joe.

Brett walked slowly as he made his way up the mountain. Callie called out, "You have to pick up the speed, Brett."

Brett's voice trembled as he confessed, "I'm afraid of heights." He looked down at his feet as he spoke. He didn't want to see how far they had climbed up the mountain, or he wouldn't be able to move.

"It's okay," Callie reassured Brett. "You can go at your own pace. I'm sorry I tried to rush you."

Brett took a deep breath as he made his way up the mountain. When the others stopped to soak in the views atop the mountain's peak, Brett just concentrated on making his way down.

"I see the taiga!" Joe exclaimed as he stood on the top of the mountain. "I'm so glad I was right. We are almost there."

Brett wanted to race down the side of the mountain and sprint to the taiga, but he decided it would be best to keep at the same pace and stare at his feet until he reached the bottom. Once he did, he followed the others toward the taiga. As they reached the icy biome, the scenic snow-topped hilly terrain overwhelmed Brett. "Wow," he marveled. "This is stunning."

"Do you see that?" asked Callie, pointing ahead.

"Yes," said Laura. "There's a stage."

There was a large stage set up in the middle of the taiga. The stage was made of snow. A person dressed in a navy snowsuit stood on the stage, and various people stood behind him. They could hear the person in the snowsuit, who introduced himself as the new mayor, call out, "We have more all-stars," and there was loud applause from the audience.

The first thing Brett noticed was how cold he felt. A shiver raced down his spine, and as he looked at the crowd standing by the stage, he wondered if he was dressed appropriately. Everyone was wearing coats, hats, and gloves, while he wore a blue T-shirt with a hole in it. His arms were covered in goose bumps. He looked over at Joe. His blue hair had icicles forming in it, but he seemed warm in his black leather jacket.

Brett didn't have time to add a jacket to his skin. Before he knew it, he was being invited up on the stage and people were applauding his introduction.

"We have Brett building a farm for us," announced the mayor. "And his coworker, Joe. They will create the first farm for Hillsdale."

The mayor continued, "We also have Poppy building an ice castle and an igloo."

The crowd applauded Poppy. The mayor introduced Callie and Laura, who were also greeted with enthusiasm. "We have accumulated some of the most talented people in the Overworld to create Hillsdale, a wintery community. I know all of you snow lovers are grateful that these people will be building your homes and creating a substantial farm."

As the mayor spoke, Brett realized that this wasn't anything sinister. They had called everyone there to build a new community. After his experience of going back in time and being there for the founding of Meadow Mews, he was excited now to help build a new community. He was also thrilled to meet all of these other important people from around the Overworld. He watched Poppy chat with a fellow builder whom she always wanted to meet. He looked around the stage and spotted Harold. Harold was one of the most prominent farmers in the Overworld. Brett had only heard about Harold's farms and had always wanted to see them. He didn't have a chance to walk over to Harold because the mayor called everyone off the stage.

"It's time for us to begin," said the mayor as he broke everyone into smaller groups.

Brett was happy to see Harold joining their group, which was just the three of them. The mayor led them to a stretch of icy land and said, "This is your canvas. Create a farm that can sustain this new village, and we will provide you each with fifty emeralds."

Brett didn't even know they were going to be paid for the project and was very excited. When the mayor left, Brett and Joe introduced themselves, and Harold said, "I usually work alone. I will try to tolerate you guys, but I'm not going to lie, it's not going to be easy for me. I like to make my own decisions, and if you guys get in my way, I will fight you."

It was hard to meet one of his idols and then realize that he wasn't as nice as Brett had imagined.

"Can we try to work together?" Brett reasoned with Harold.

Harold stood silently. There was an uncomfortable pause until Poppy came toward them.

"Look over there!" She smiled and pointed to a spot adjacent to the farm. "That's where I'm going to build my ice castle. This means we can create an igloo and room together." She looked at Harold. "Do you want to live in the igloo with us?"

Harold shrugged, pulled out a torch, and began to melt the snow without saying a word.

5

ALONE IN THE FUTURE

Brett melted ice with a torch as he chuckled to himself. It was very ironic that he often day-dreamed about creating an ideal farm with Harold and now that he was working with him, it was an awful experience. They had been in Hillsdale for a little less than a week, and Harold hadn't spoken a word unless it was to tell Brett that he was wrong. Harold even had the audacity to take the room that Brett had built for himself in the igloo.

"I don't know if I am going to make it another day," confessed Brett. "I might just have to go back to Meadow Mews. Harold is impossible."

"I know he's hard to work with, but you can't just stop working on the farm. We made a promise, and besides, I want the emeralds," said Joe.

"You can stay and get the emeralds. I can leave. I think you know enough to work on the farm alone with Harold," said Brett. "But I don't think I can keep this up."

Joe suggested, "Perhaps you should take a walk and just be alone for a little while. Maybe when you come back, you'll feel better. I know Harold isn't easy to work with, but I don't think it's worth giving up the job."

Brett wondered if Joe was right. Maybe he was overreacting. He decided to take Joe's advice and bundled up in a black coat and took a walk toward Poppy's ice castle.

He saw Poppy, Callie, and Laura hard at work on the castle. In less than a week, they had built the entire base of the castle. They were completing the job in record time. Poppy had mentioned they worked well together and that was the reason they were being so productive. He was in the exact opposite situation, and he secretly envied Poppy's relationship with her coworkers.

Brett waved to Poppy, but she didn't see him. She was distracted with building the side of the castle. As he approached the castle, Brett slipped on the ice and fell into an icy hole. He had thought Hillsdale was cold, but the frigid air in the hole was brutal. He shivered, and this feeling was all too familiar to him. Brett remembered falling down the hole in Meadow Mews and landing in the past. He had no idea where he was going to wind up, but he knew he was in a portal. He recalled the sensation of feeling as if he were falling forever. Although he had experienced this before, it still made him nervous. His heart beat rapidly, and his forehead was covered in sweat that was slowly transforming into

ice. He was terrified. He was trapped, and this time he
didn't even have Joe with him. He was alone.

As Brett tumbled deeper in the hole, he hoped
Poppy had spotted him fall down the hole; but as he
traveled on this seemingly endless journey, he didn't
hear anybody call out his name. The idea that he
could be trapped on his own in a strange place terrified
him—it scared him more than climbing up a mountain. His teeth were chattering, and he wasn't sure if it
was a reaction to the cold or to terror.

Thump! Brett landed on a grassy patch. He stood up.
He wasn't in the cold biome, but was standing next to
a lush oak tree.

"Brett!" He heard Nancy call out his name.

"Nancy," Brett said as he rushed over to her. "I
thought you were on a treasure hunt. Is it over?"

"Treasure hunt? I haven't hunted for treasure in
ages, you know that?" She looked at Brett. "It's weird,
but I saw you two minutes ago, and you weren't wearing a coat. Are you okay? You don't look well. It looks
like you've been sweating."

Brett looked around, and everything looked familiar. He saw the farm in the distance. He was in Meadow
Mews, but he wasn't certain what time period he had
landed in. "I'm okay," said Brett. "I just want to go
home and lie down."

Brett walked toward his home, and Nancy called
out, "Why are you walking that way? You haven't lived
in that direction in years. Are you sure you're okay?"

"I'm in the future." These words fell from Brett's mouth, and he regretted saying them because he wasn't sure how to explain the situation to Nancy. She had no idea that he had traveled to the past with Joe.

"I think you're sick," said Nancy. "There is a flu going around. It actually affected some of the animals too. I bet you have it," Nancy suggested. "Let me walk you home. I'm worried about you."

Brett followed Nancy to his new home. She led him down a tree-lined path, but Brett didn't see any house. "Where are we?"

"We're home." She stopped in front of a large oak tree.

"Where?" asked Brett. "I don't see a house."

Nancy pulled a potion from her inventory. "Here, take this potion of healing. I think it will help you."

Brett sipped the potion, which gave him an energy boost, but it didn't help him. He was still so confused, and even though he despised every day he had worked with Harold, he wished he could get back to Hillsdale and finish the farm. He actually considered asking Nancy if she recalled that period in time and if she remembered how it turned out, but instead he asked again, "Where is the house?"

"Oh, Brett." She pointed to stairs against the tree. "Look up."

Brett stared at a large tree house. "Wow, that's very nice."

"It is." Her blue eyes filled with tears when she said, "Poppy built it for you before she—" but she choked up and couldn't continue.

"Before she what?"

"You know what I mean, but this isn't the time to talk about the past. It's time for us to get you to bed," she said as she climbed up the stairs and led Brett to the tree house. But when they reached the top of the stairs, Nancy let out a gasp and screamed, "Who are you? And how did you replicate my friend's skin?"

6

YOU LOOK THE SAME

Brett had known this moment was going to happen, but he still wasn't prepared for it. He had imagined what it would be like for his old self to walk up the stairs to the tree house dressed in a black coat. He wanted to greet him and tell him what had happened in the decades since he had fallen down the hole in Hillsdale, but he also knew this was a sign. They had no time to talk about the past, because the minute Brett arrived in his house, confusing Nancy, the town of Meadow Mews would be filled with creepers. He also knew that he would disappear, and the old Brett would never know where he wound up. He wanted to tell his old self everything, but there was no time.

Kaboom! A loud explosion ripped through the tree house, knocking Nancy and Brett to the ground.

Nancy looked through the rubble. "Where is the real Brett?" she hollered.

"I'm the real Brett," Brett reassured her as he took off the thick black coat and placed it in his inventory. The heat from the explosion made him overheat, and he had to take it off. Once he removed the jacket, he looked like the Brett that Nancy had always known.

"If you're the real Brett, who was the person who looked just like you in the tree house?" asked Nancy.

"It's complicated," said Brett, "but we're the same person, and I have to find him."

"Are you trying to tell me that you're some kind of time traveler?" questioned Nancy.

"Yes," said Brett, but he didn't have time to explain because, within seconds, the streets of Meadow Mews were flooded with creepers.

"What's going on?" asked Nancy.

"I don't know," Brett's voice shook. He had never seen this many creepers in his life, and as he pulled a bow and arrow from his inventory and tried to shoot the explosive green mobs, the sky grew dark, and lightning struck the area around the creepers. A blue aura surrounded the creepers.

"Oh no!" hollered Nancy. "Now they are charged creepers."

Nancy tried to battle the creepers, but she had only two hearts when a charged creeper detonated next to her, and she was destroyed.

Brett grabbed a potion of strength and sipped it as he shot arrows at the creepers. Rain fell on the ground, and Brett's feet were drenched in the puddles that filled the grassy ground. He wondered what had happened to the Brett from his future. Brett looked back at the debris from the tree house, but he didn't see his future self.

"Brett!" he called out. It felt strange calling out his name. There was no response. Brett shot more arrows at the creepers, and when the final creeper was destroyed, the rain had stopped. Brett dashed into town. He spotted Nancy in the distance.

"Nancy," Brett called out.

Nancy stopped. "I don't trust you," she confessed. "I don't believe your tale of time travel. I think you've destroyed Brett and stolen his skin."

"I promise," said Brett, "I would never do such a thing."

As they spoke, Helen and Franklin walked down the street, and Brett called out to them. He told Nancy, "They will believe me. They know that I traveled to the past, so they understand that I have the ability to travel through time."

Nancy said, "Well, you did know that I was once a treasure hunter. Not many people know that about me." She was beginning to believe Brett.

Franklin and Helen walked over to them, but before they could talk, the sky grew dark, and more creepers spawned in the streets.

"What is happening?" asked Helen as she pulled a bow and arrow from her inventory and shot the creepers.

Thunder shook the town, and lightning struck a crop of creepers. "More charged creepers," screamed Nancy. "How can we get this to stop?"

"I think we're being attacked," said Franklin as he splashed potions on the creepers.

As the rain soaked the ground, Brett tried not to slip as he fought the creepers. While shooting an arrow, he felt a pain radiate down his arm and turned around to see a skeleton aiming another arrow in his direction.

Nancy called out, "Zombies! I see zombies!"

The village streets were filled with charged creepers, zombies, and skeletons, and Brett wondered where he'd respawn if he was destroyed. He hoped that he'd wind up in the cold biome. He decided to let this collection of beasts destroy him. As he put down his bow and arrow, Nancy looked over at him. "What are you doing? Why aren't you helping us?"

Brett fumbled with his words. "Because I . . ."

Nancy screamed, "Pick up your bow and arrow and fight."

The rain stopped, the last creeper was destroyed, and Brett stood face-to-face with Nancy, who wanted to know why he wasn't battling the hostile mobs like the rest of them.

"I wanted to be destroyed," confessed Brett. "I thought I might respawn in the past, where I belong."

"Were you only thinking about yourself?" asked Nancy. "What about Meadow Mews? It was being destroyed by mobs."

Helen and Franklin stood by and listened. Helen asked, "Brett, are you not in the right time period?"

"Yes," said Brett. "Remember when this happened

to me before? I was in the middle of the clash of the Withers."

"I do remember that, but you stayed with us and helped us battle the Withers. The way you acted just now doesn't seem like the Brett that we know at all," said Helen.

"Yes, the Brett that we know would have battled alongside of us," added Franklin.

"I don't trust you," said Nancy. "Ever since you arrived, we have been under attack."

"Is that true?" asked Franklin.

"Yes," Nancy confirmed. "He showed up in Meadow Mews, and now we are in a battle."

Brett defended himself. "I'm sorry. I did help you in the other attack earlier, but I am tired, and I wanted to go back home. You guys recall how I stood by you in the Wither battle? But this time, I don't think I can. I want to go home."

Brett hoped his speech would convince them that he was actually who he said he was, but it didn't work. Nancy pulled out her enchanted diamond sword and pressed it against Brett's unarmored arm.

"Prove to us that you are really Brett," she said as she pressed the sword deeper into the flesh of his arm. He was overwhelmed with pain, and he lost a heart.

7
TRUTH OR DARE

"I'm telling you the truth," Brett cried. "I'm really Brett. What do you want me to say to convince you? I can tell you about going back in the past and helping Helen and Franklin defeat Withers and the story of Grant's disappearance."

"Don't hurt him," said Helen. "I think he's telling the truth."

Nancy backed away and handed Brett a potion to regenerate his strength. He was weak from the sword depleting his heart. Brett thanked her as he took a sip.

"I am telling the truth," said Brett as he finished the potion. "And I want you guys to know that I don't want to be here. I went through this before, and I stuck around to help Meadow Mews, but now I just want to go back home. I'm not supposed to know my future."

"We understand how you feel. In fact, if I remember

correctly, you felt the same way when you went back in time and helped us settle Meadow Mews."

"I know, but this time is different." Brett paused and asked, "Where's Poppy? I want to see her."

"Poppy is—" Nancy said and then stopped. "She doesn't live here anymore."

"Where is she?" questioned Brett.

"It doesn't matter," Helen said. "You want to go back home, and we're apparently under attack. This is not the time to track down an old friend."

"But Poppy's my best friend," said Brett.

Franklin asked, "Where is your future self?"

"He's missing," explained Nancy. "We haven't seen him since someone blew up his tree house with TNT."

"Who would do that?" asked Helen.

"I don't know who my enemies are in the future. Do I have any?" asked Brett. "Would Poppy know?"

"We told you," said Helen. "Poppy doesn't live here anymore. You haven't seen her in a while."

Brett couldn't imagine not seeing Poppy. She had been his best friend for as long as he could remember. He wondered what happened to their friendship in the future, but he didn't have the time to ask questions, because a loud explosion was heard in the distance.

Kaboom! Smoke rose in the town. Franklin shouted, "Oh no! The castle! Poppy's castle."

The gang sprinted into town. Brett spotted familiar faces in the distance. He saw Lou the Blacksmith and Heather the Librarian as they raced toward the smoke.

Heather stood by the castle and cried, "Someone

is destroying the town. This castle was a piece of our history."

"And they also blew up Brett's tree house," said Nancy.

Lou looked at Brett. "You must be so upset. Poppy built that for you before she left. You always talk about the tree house."

Brett wanted to ask where Poppy was living, but before he could speak, the sky grew dark again, and creepers flooded the narrow village streets. Brett knew someone must have been using command blocks to create these storms and the creepers, and they were also using TNT to blow up the buildings in Meadow Mews. He wondered who would want to destroy this flourishing town.

Brett shot arrows at the green silent killers, but no matter how many creepers he was able to obliterate, more spawned. The rain was pounding down, and zombies lumbered through the town, ripping doors off hinges and transforming innocent villagers into the living dead. Everyone in the town was battling the mobs, and Brett saw a slew of familiar faces. As he destroyed a creeper that exploded inches from his feet, he smiled. He was happy that most of the people he knew had stayed in Meadow Mews and that they all seemed to still get along. Of course, he wondered what had happened to Poppy, and resolved to unmask that mystery. He knew that knowing a lot about his future had the potential to disrupt the time period he was living in, but if there was information that would help him stay in contact with Poppy, he had to use it.

"Help!" Franklin hollered as three creepers and a zombie surrounded him. Brett rushed to Franklin, trading in his bow and arrow for a diamond sword and a bottle of potion. He splashed potion to weaken the zombie and creepers and then slammed his sword into the zombie, destroying the horrid-smelling beast. The creepers were harder to battle, and he jumped back as he struck them with a sword.

"Thanks," Franklin said as he destroyed the final creeper.

The rain stopped as quickly as it had started, and the hostile mobs vanished. When the sun shone down on them, the townspeople walked over to see what had happened to the castle.

"Who would do something like this?" Nancy asked the crowd.

"Are there any suspects?" a man in a blue hat called out.

"No," said Helen. "This has just begun."

"I find it strange that this person is targeting Poppy's work," said Brett. "They blew up the tree house and now the castle. We should try to protect Poppy's other buildings before they're destroyed."

The crowd turned to Brett with a collective perplexed look.

"What other buildings?" asked Heather the Librarian.

Brett looked out past the castle where Poppy had built a skyscraper, but it was missing. "Where's the skyscraper?"

Lou the Blacksmith questioned, "Are you feeling okay? That's been gone for years."

Heather said, "Those were the only two buildings left after the . . ." She stopped talking as she started to cry.

Brett knew he had to learn about the past to save the future.

8

THE NITWIT

The sun was setting, and Nancy offered Brett a room in her house. Brett followed Nancy back to her stone house in a lush area of Meadow Mews. They had to walk through a path of leaves to enter the door. When they were in the living room, Brett got up the courage to ask about Poppy. "I know that I'm not supposed to know too much about the future because it might impact the way things turn out, but I have to know what happened to Poppy."

"Do I really have to tell you? Obviously, you will go back in time, because there were two of you when I found you, and I think it's probably best for you to know what is happening now, but not what came between your time period and this one."

"Okay, but can you answer this question? Did Poppy have any enemies? Is there someone who might have wanted to erase her existence from Meadow

Mews? That might be why they targeted her last two structures," said Brett.

"I will tell you that Poppy hasn't been in Meadow Mews in a long time, so I don't know why someone would even think about erasing her memory here. She was a great person and everyone liked her, but. . . ." Nancy censored herself.

"I don't think I can help you guys if I don't know the entire story," Brett complained.

"Maybe you aren't here to solve the problem. Maybe you're simply a soldier, and you will help us battle these creepers," said Nancy.

Brett understood what Nancy was saying, but he knew there had to be a reason that he was chosen to travel through time. He felt he was brought into the future to save the past. If Nancy wasn't going to tell him about the history between his time period and hers, he would go to the library in the morning and talk to Heather the Librarian.

"I'm going to bed," he yawned.

Nancy led Brett down a long hall and opened the door to a small room with a chest and a bed. He thanked her and climbed into bed. As he pulled the wool covers over himself, he hoped he'd awake and this would all be a dream.

In the morning, when the sun shone through the tiny window, he knew that it wasn't a dream. He was stuck in the future. He jumped out of bed, sipped milk, ate a cookie that was in Nancy's kitchen, and headed to the village to go to the library.

Brett was outside of the village when a villager with striking green eyes, a bald head, and a green robe approached him.

"Hi." Brett had never seen a villager who dressed in a green robe. He wondered what the newcomer had to trade. "What's your name?"

"Bob," said the man in the green robe. "What, you don't recognize me, Brett?"

"What do you trade?" asked Brett.

"Nothing. I have no interest in trading. You know that, Brett. We hang out all the time," replied Bob.

"Don't you want emeralds?" questioned Brett.

"Why?" asked Bob.

"All of the villagers want emeralds. That is why we trade with them all the time," explained Brett, who was annoyed. He didn't want to waste time trying to explain something to this nitwit when he had to get to the library. He needed to get any book he could on the history of Meadow Mews.

"You know me. I don't like emeralds. I just like walking around and talking to people," said Bob the Nitwit.

"Well, if you don't have anything to trade, I'm afraid I have to go," Brett told him.

"Why? We can hang out. Since I don't trade anything, I don't have a job. This means I have loads of free time. I love just hanging out with people and spending the day chatting. We've spent mornings talking."

Brett wished he could live a life of leisure, but he had to find a way to get back home, and he also had to help the town with the creeper invasion. He was shocked that his future self was so friendly with someone who seemed to lack motivation. Brett loved to talk to people who had different ambitions about how they carried out their jobs. This reminded him that he wanted to find out what happened to Joe. Brett knew Joe didn't live in Meadow Mews, but maybe there was something in the history books about Joe's farming in Farmer's Bay.

"So can we hang out this morning?" asked Bob.

Brett excused himself and bolted to the library. He could hear Bob question, "Why do you want to read?"

Bob was a Nitwit. He didn't read. He didn't work. He just existed. Brett told himself that he would be bored of that existence in a day. It seemed rather pointless. As he hurried into the library, Heather the Librarian greeted him.

"I met the strangest man on the way here," said Brett. "He said we're friends. His name is Bob."

"You hang out with Bob all the time. He loves to watch you farm, and you feed him apples," said Heather. "Why didn't you recognize him?"

Brett knew that Heather, a person who spent her life surrounded by books and stories, would be someone who would understand his story about his ability to time travel. She might even have a few books about time travel that might offer him suggestions on how to get back home. He told Heather how he fell down a hole in the cold biome and how he arrived in the future.

"I've heard stories about how you once traveled back in time during the clash of the Withers," said Heather.

"Really?" asked Brett.

"Joe told me about it a long time ago. Before he went back to Farmer's Bay," she replied.

"Do you still see Joe?" asked Brett.

"He comes by sometimes. He helped you expand the farm last year," she said.

Brett was happy that Joe was still around. He was about to ask her about Poppy when she handed him a stack of books.

"You've missed out on a huge chunk of time," she explained as she handed him the books. "I don't know if you reading these books is the best idea. I'm sure it will impact the future, but I think the more you know, the better off you are, so feel free to stay here all day and read."

Brett flipped through the books and opened a chapter about architecture and building. The first name he saw was Poppy's. His jaw dropped as he read about Poppy.

9

CAUGHT UP WITH THE CREEPERS

"I have to find her," Brett said, but there was nobody around to hear him. He read the rest of the entry to see if there were any clues to where she might be hiding.

Poppy, one of the most renowned builders in the Overworld, was hired to build an amusement park on Mushroom Island. She left Meadow Mews but never arrived on the island and was reported missing. There was a large-scale search for Poppy, but the boat she traveled on and her companions Callie and Laura were never heard from again. After a six-month search, it was declared they were gone from the Overworld.

Brett reread the entry several times. He couldn't believe it. He had to go back in time and warn them. He couldn't believe this had happened years ago. How could he have ever stopped looking for Poppy? What type of friend was he? He jogged to Nancy's house. She was standing outside picking apples from a tree.

"Poppy is missing? Why didn't you tell me she was lost at sea?" asked Brett.

"I knew this would happen." Nancy placed the apples in her inventory as she spoke. "You went to the library. You weren't there when she went missing. It's easy to read about it in a book, but when you live it, you know the real story."

"Tell me the real story," said Brett.

"We looked for Poppy for a lot longer than they say in the history books. You never gave up. You spent every possible free day searching for her. You lived at sea for an entire year. You searched every underwater monument. You traveled around the Overworld tracking down anyone you thought might have trapped her somewhere. You went to every new town that was being built to see if she had wound up there and was building. You wondered if she had amnesia and had lost her memory. You were a changed person. It was kind of nice having the old you back. I knew once you found out about this, you'd become obsessed."

Brett said, "I have to find her." He theorized, "Maybe that is why I got to travel into the future."

"Maybe when you get back home, you can warn Poppy and her friends," said Nancy.

"Yes," said Brett, "I have to. How am I going to get back home?"

"I don't know," said Nancy. "I was thinking of ways

to get you back home. I know there is a cave outside of town and weird things have happened in there."

"Like what?"

Nancy rattled off a list of strange occurrences. "Diamonds appear there all the time, people say there are no mobs in the cave, there is a rumor that an old man lives in the stronghold and he grants wishes . . ."

Brett stopped her. "Wishes? Really? That seems pretty unbelievable, but I'd like to see him."

"I'll take you there," said Nancy.

As she led Brett to the cave, the skies darkened again. This time they weren't simply being attacked by a glob of green explosive creatures, but by the Ender Dragon, which spawned in the sky above them and shot a fiery bomb from its mouth.

"An Ender Dragon!" screamed Nancy. "I haven't seen one in years."

Franklin and Helen raced toward them clutching bows and arrows and aimed at the muscular gray beast that flew above them.

The Ender Dragon swept down and breathed a fiery ball that landed on Brett's legs, leaving him with one heart. He went to grab a potion from his inventory to replenish his energy, but when he turned around, a creeper exploded behind him. He awoke in Nancy's house. He could see his friends battling the Ender Dragon from the window.

"Help!" Helen screamed.

Brett tore from the house and shot an arrow at the weakened dragon, destroying the beast.

"Good job!" exclaimed Nancy.

A portal to the End spawned outside of her house. Brett avoided falling down that portal. He had gone to enough dimensions he'd never intended to visit. He wanted to meet the man in the cave, the one who granted wishes. He knew that this was probably something his future self had done, and his wish obviously hadn't come true, because Poppy was still missing.

"I want to see the man who lives in the stronghold in the cave," said Brett.

"I'll take you there," said Nancy.

"That man is a little nutty," warned Helen.

"Do you want to go with us?" asked Brett.

Helen and Franklin agreed to go with them. They walked toward the cave, but they passed two block-carrying Endermen. Brett tried not to lock eyes with the creatures, but he thought he saw a creeper from the corner of his eye, and he accidentally glanced in the direction of the Endermen. One of the Endermen began to shriek and teleported toward him.

"What am I going to do?" screamed Brett.

"Run!" exclaimed Nancy. "Run to the water."

Brett knew there was a small pond near his farm. He sprinted, but the Enderman was close behind him. He picked up speed and then jumped into the pond. The Enderman followed him. He was safe.

"Are you okay?" asked Nancy as she helped him out of the pond.

"I will be once my wish comes true," he said and followed her and the others to the cave.

10

FINDING YOURSELF

"I thought the cave was right here," said Nancy as she walked farther outside of Meadow Mews, but she couldn't find the entrance.

"Isn't it north of the village?" asked Franklin.

"No, this is where it is," declared Nancy.

"It can't be," said Helen. "A cave can't move. You must be thinking of a different spot."

Nancy was distressed. "If it's not here, I have no idea where it might be. Do you guys know where it is? I can't be the only person who has been there."

Helen and Franklin admitted they had never been to the cave but had just heard about it. As they spoke, the nitwit walked up and asked, "Can I help you guys?"

"Bob," Brett waved him away, "not now."

"What are you up to? Do you want me to leave?" asked Bob.

"Yes," Brett replied curtly.

"Don't be rude," Nancy said to Brett.

"I'm sorry, Bob," Brett said, "but we have to find the cave. I need to see the man who grants wishes."

"I know the way. I've spent many afternoons chatting with him. He's great. He knows everything about alchemy. His name is Kurt," said Bob.

"Really? You know the way?" Brett was shocked.

Bob led them through a path outside of town and into an area thick with leaves. He cleared the way and showed them the cave's entrance.

"Here it is," said Bob. "Kurt lives in the stronghold. I'll introduce you guys."

As they walked into the cave, Brett felt bad that he had been rude to Bob. He said, "Bob, I'm sorry if you thought I was rude, but I haven't been myself lately."

"No worries," said Bob casually. "We all get that way." Bob led them down a dimly lit hallway and turned around when he heard Brett's sword brushing against the cave wall. "You don't need your sword here. This is a magical cave. You'll never see a hostile mob here."

"I don't believe in magic," said Brett.

"Really?" Helen seemed surprised. "I find it strange that someone who has the ability to travel through time doesn't believe in magic."

"Well, I don't," Brett explained. "There has to be a logical reason I fell down those portals."

Bob wasn't listening to their conversation. He was walking down the dimly lit hall. "Does anybody have a torch?"

Brett had many torches because he had planned to use them to melt the snow when he built a farm in Hillsdale. He felt a pang of sadness when he thought of his friends in Hillsdale. They must be worried wondering where he went. Brett pulled out a torch and placed it on the wall of the stronghold so they would have light.

The light from the torch helped them find the door. "We're here," said Bob as he opened the door to the stronghold. Before he could lead them through the stronghold, there was a loud explosion. They turned around to see Helen destroyed by a creeper.

Two creepers silently made their way down the narrow hallway. Brett sighed. "I thought there weren't any hostile mobs in this cave."

"We've never heard of there being any in the cave," said Franklin.

"Just because you never heard of hostile mobs being here doesn't mean it's true," said Brett.

Brett traded in his diamond sword for a bow and arrow and shot an arrow at the creeper that moved toward them, destroying both creepers.

"Good job," said Helen, who reappeared at the end of the hall. "I TPed here as fast as I could."

Brett said, "I told you there's no such thing as magic." He pulled out his diamond sword and readjusted his armor.

Bob opened the door to the stronghold. This time Helen, Franklin, Nancy, and Brett were carrying diamond swords. Bob led them down the stairs and toward a room with a bookcase. A man with a gray beard wore a blue hat, a denim jacket, and a green shirt and stood next to the bookcase. He smiled when he saw Bob. "Bob, my old friend, to what do I owe the pleasure of your company?"

"My friend needs help, and you're the only person I know who can help him," explained Bob.

Brett was shocked when Kurt focused his green eyes right on him. "You're the one in need of help, aren't you?" questioned Kurt. Then Kurt looked at the others. "Something is not right in Meadow Mews. This stronghold isn't safe anymore. There are problems happening, and we must stop them."

"Problems?" asked Helen.

"Watch out!" Nancy screamed as two creepers floated toward Helen. She dodged away from the creepers, and Kurt pulled out a bow and arrow and destroyed them with two arrows.

"It's been a long time since I had to fight a hostile mob," he said, "but it looks like I haven't lost my touch."

"You're a strong warrior," said Bob.

"But Bob, you know I don't want to fight. That is why I settled in this magical stronghold. I didn't want to live a life where I was constantly battling hostile mobs. I wanted peace and quiet, but now there is a sinister force at work, and it has flooded Meadow Mews with creepers." Bob looked at Brett. "And you, Brett, must stop it."

"How do you know my name?" asked Brett.

"I know you," Kurt said. "I've always known you."

"What does that mean?" questioned Brett. He didn't like the cryptic response.

"It means that you were sent here for a reason," said Kurt.

"But how do I stop the creeper invasion?" asked Brett.

"You will find a way. Just don't give up," said Kurt.

"Give me a clue. I don't know what to do. Help me. Guide me." Brett was on the verge of begging. He hadn't asked to be in charge of saving the future of Meadow Mews. He wanted to go back in time. He wanted to warn Poppy that she would go missing along with Callie and Laura.

"The clue is within you. You can guide yourself," said Kurt.

"I'm honored that you believe in me, but I don't think I'm up for the job. And I also want to find my missing friend." Brett's eyes filled with tears.

Kurt hollered, "Oh no! Watch out!"

The cave was crowded with creepers. There was no time to talk; they had to battle.

11

A BELIEVER

As Brett aimed his arrow at a creeper, destroying the explosive green mob, he thought about magic. He wished it did exist. He wanted to be saved. He wanted to be reunited with Poppy. He wanted to know how to save Meadow Mews from the creeper invasion. He looked back at Kurt, who was battling the creepers. He had so many questions for Kurt, but he knew the answers wouldn't satisfy him. He had to figure this out on his own. The final creeper was destroyed, and the group let out a collective sigh of relief and grabbed potions and milk from their inventories to regain their strength.

Kurt said, "This cave is no place for you guys. Meadow Mews is in trouble, and you have to be in town trying to stop this invasion."

"You were supposed to help us," said Brett.

"This isn't a job for me," Kurt replied. "You don't need answers; you need action."

"Can you help me find Poppy?" asked Brett.

"Please focus on finding your friend later. This is the time to win a battle that won't stop unless you start taking action," Kurt said. "I have nothing else to say to you. It's best if you leave."

The group stood by Kurt and didn't move.

Bob looked at them. "Didn't you hear Kurt? He wants us to leave, and we better get going."

Brett reluctantly followed Bob out of the stronghold, but they couldn't move very far because the cave was inundated by another creeper invasion.

"What is happening?" asked Nancy. "This has to stop."

Brett blurted out, "We will make it stop." He was shocked at his confidence. He was only confident when he was farming, but now he must lead them to a victory. It was his only way to get back home.

The creepers were packed in the narrow hallway. Brett took a deep breath as he stared at their black eyes while they walked down the hall without making a sound. Two creepers exploded next to Nancy, destroying her. Brett shot arrows, but it felt like a pointless act because there were so many creepers, and it didn't seem possible to destroy them all.

He shot another arrow, but a creeper approached him and exploded, and Brett awoke in Nancy's house.

"Brett," Nancy called out.

"Yes." He sat up in the bed and sipped a potion to regain his health.

"There's someone here to see you," said Nancy. "We're in the living room."

Brett couldn't imagine who would be here to see him. He walked into Nancy's living room and smiled when he saw Joe.

"Joe! How are you? The last time I saw you, we were building an ice farm in Hillsdale."

"You have no idea how long ago that was," said Joe.

"Did it turn out okay?" asked Brett.

"You'll find out when you go back home. I don't want to tell too much about your past because it could impact your future. Nancy told me you already know about Poppy."

"Yes." Brett stared down at the ground. He couldn't look at Joe. It was too painful to talk about Poppy.

"I'm here because I think I can help you battle the person who is behind this creeper invasion."

"Really? How?"

Joe said, "It's an old enemy, and when I say old, I mean very old. The person who is behind these attacks is Connor."

"Connor?" asked Brett. "You mean the person who fought with Grant and tried to destroy Meadow Mews when it was first founded? I thought he was gone and that battle was over."

"So did everyone, until I spotted him in Farmer's Bay. Then I heard about the attacks on Meadow Mews, and I knew he was behind the creeper invasion," said Joe.

"You don't have any proof. Are you just basing this off of the fact that you saw him on the streets of Farmer's Bay?"

"Well," Joe stuttered, "I mean, yes."

"Did you even speak to him?" asked Brett.

"No," Joe replied.

"I don't think we should jump to conclusions. I think we should question him. I will travel to Farmer's Bay with you," said Brett.

"There's no need," said Joe. "He's already here in Meadow Mews."

"How do you know?" asked Nancy.

"I saw him in the village. He was visiting Lou the Blacksmith," said Joe.

"We have to head to the village," said Brett as he adjusted his armor and pulled his enchanted diamond sword from his inventory.

"What about our friends?" asked Nancy. "Shouldn't we TP back to the cave and save them from the creeper invasion?"

"Yes," said Brett, "we should do that first." But Brett wasn't sure this was the correct response. He was worried about his friends, but he also knew that if they questioned Connor and he was responsible for this new battle, they could get him to stop the creeper attacks, and they would not only save their friends, but everybody else in the town.

Brett didn't have to make a decision. Franklin,

Helen, and Kurt stood outside Nancy's house and opened the door to the living room.

Helen said, "The cave is uninhabitable. It seems like it's a breeding ground for creepers."

"A monster spawner!" shouted Brett. "I bet that's where he is keeping the spawner."

"He?" questioned Franklin.

"Who are you talking about?" asked Helen.

"Connor," said Brett. "He's back."

"Seriously?" Helen was shocked.

"But we can't jump to conclusions that he is behind these attacks. Although I do find it strange that he reappeared at this point in time, we can't say he's guilty of creating the attack on Meadow Mews," explained Brett.

"Why else would he be here?" asked Franklin. "Think about all of the trouble he caused us when we were founding this town. We have to find out why he came back here. We never thought we'd see him again."

"That's true," said Brett. "But we need to find him first."

The group hurried out of Nancy's house and headed to the town. Brett wondered how they could approach Connor without making him feel as if he were under attack. His mind raced as they made their way toward the town and spotted Connor in the center of the village. When Connor saw them, he quickly constructed a portal to the Nether, and by the time they reached him, he was surrounded by purple mist.

12

NETHER LEAVE

"What should we do?" asked Brett. His blond hair fell into his eyes as he headed toward the portal.

"Follow him! Go on the portal!" instructed Helen.

Kurt said, "I can't believe I have to go to the Nether. I haven't been there in ages."

"You haven't been out of your cave in a long time," said Helen.

The gang hopped onto the portal, emerging in the middle of the Nether, but before they could find Connor, they were under attack. A barrage of fireballs shot at them, overwhelming the group. Several fireballs landed on their unarmored limbs and destroyed Franklin.

"Franklin!" Helen screamed.

Brett, Joe, and Nancy shot arrows at the ghasts that flew above them. The ghasts swooped down to unleash deadly fireballs.

"This is worse than the creeper invasion. I've never seen this many ghasts in the Nether," Brett said breathlessly as he shot another arrow at a beast with striking red eyes and a high-pitched shriek. The sounds emanating from the ghasts were deafening, and Brett wanted to cover his ears, but he couldn't. He had to concentrate and focus on the ghasts. He destroyed one ghast, but he was unable to grab the ghast tear it dropped on the netherrack ground because it would leave him vulnerable to an attack from the other ghasts.

I'll get it later, he told himself. He shot another arrow, destroying a second ghast. From the corner of his eye, he could see Joe destroy another ghast. He had to admit that he liked being reunited with Joe. Even though he was in the midst of a battle to save the future of Meadow Mews, he was glad that he had his friend and partner by his side and he could battle alongside him.

"I see Connor!" Helen called out as she battled a ghast. A fireball from the white fiery beast nearly hit her leg. She pulled back and steadied herself as she shot another arrow and destroyed the ghast.

"We have to get him!" said Nancy.

"How?" Joe asked. There were still six ghasts circling in the skies above them. "We can't leave unless we destroy these ghasts."

Kurt fumbled with his bow and arrow. He hadn't pulled a weapon from his inventory in years, and in the past day, he had used all the weapons he thought he'd never touch again. He looked at the ghast and shot the arrow, and he marveled when he saw that he had destroyed the ghast with a single hit.

"Good job, Kurt," Nancy commended him.

Helen destroyed a ghast and then Nancy destroyed another one, leading them to believe this was going to be easier than they thought. Brett said, "We just have four more ghasts. Let's try to keep our eyes on Connor. We don't want to lose sight of him."

"That's impossible," said Helen as she shot an arrow at a ghast and missed because she was too busy focusing on Connor.

Two zombie pigmen walked toward them, and Brett tried not to engage. He wanted to end the battle with the ghasts and not to start another one with these undead pigs.

Kurt destroyed a ghast, and another ghast tear fell to the netherrack ground. "We're almost done. Just three more to go," said Kurt.

Brett was exhausted, and the battle had left him with just a few hearts left. He grabbed a potion from his inventory to replenish his energy levels, and he shot another arrow and destroyed a ghast. There were two left, and the zombie pigmen were walking closer to the group.

Helen and Joe destroyed the remaining ghasts. Without making eye contact with the zombie pigmen, the gang ran toward Connor, but they had lost him.

"I don't see him," said Helen. She pushed her long red hair behind her back. Helen stood next to a lava stream, and her hair almost blended into this crimson flow.

Joe looked in all directions and then pointed to a bridge. "Let's go up there and see if we have a better view." The gang followed him as he led them up onto the bridge.

As Kurt climbed the stairs, sweat formed on his brow. "I forgot how hot it is in the Nether. I miss the cool stronghold."

"Hopefully, we won't be here long," said Brett.

"I see him!" Helen called out.

Connor was hidden behind a cluster of mushrooms growing by the entrance to a cavern. Joe said, "Let's get him!" and the gang raced toward Connor.

As they approached Connor, Brett reminded them that they needed proof he was behind the creeper attacks in Meadow Mews. They couldn't assume he was guilty and that he was behind these attacks yet. They shouldn't jump to conclusions.

"Are you joking?" Helen questioned as they reached the entrance to the cave.

Kurt said, "I don't even know Connor, and I think he's guilty."

"Why?" asked Brett.

"I was living a peaceful existence in the stronghold until he showed up," replied Kurt.

"But that doesn't mean he is behind the attacks. Maybe he's here to stop them," suggested Brett.

"That's a nice way of looking at it, but it's very naïve," said Helen.

"I have no idea why you'd think Connor was innocent. I mean, all signs point to him being behind this attack. He showed up in town the only other time Meadow Mews has been attacked in its history," said Joe, then he paused. "You know I shouldn't talk about the history of Meadow Mews in front of Brett. He shouldn't know any more than he already does."

"Is this the only time in its history that Meadow Mews has been under attack other than the clash of the Withers?" asked Brett.

"Yes," said Helen, "and here we are confronted with Connor again. I mean, it makes sense that he is behind these attacks."

Brett understood how it might look like Connor was the one who was destroying Meadow Mews, but he still wanted more proof. At this point, all they did was speculate that he was the one who was destroying the town. As they walked into the cave, they traded in their bows and arrows for enchanted diamond swords.

A voice called out behind them, "Guys."

The group turned around and saw Franklin walking into the cave. Helen smiled. "You made it back. I am so glad."

Nancy signaled for Franklin to talk softly. She put her finger over her lips.

Franklin asked, "Is this where he is?"

"Yes," a voice shouted from deep within the cave, "and you are all my prisoners."

13

EXPLOSIONS

Brett leaped at Connor and shouted, "I'm not your prisoner!" He slammed his enchanted diamond sword into Connor's arm.

Connor splashed a potion of harming on Brett, leaving him with one heart. Connor grabbed his sword and held it against Brett's weakened body. "This is the end of Meadow Mews."

Brett asked, "Why? It's been here so long. I don't understand."

Connor laughed. "This is something I've been planning for years. Every time I hear about Meadow Mews, I am upset. I don't want this town to exist. I tried to erase it at the start, and it didn't work. I did leave, but it was always on my mind. I just don't want this town to exist."

"But people are living there. They are happy, and it's their home. How can you do this again? Didn't you learn how your actions affect others?" asked Helen.

"Helen." Connor smiled. "I can't believe I get to battle all of you again. This time, however, there is going to be a different ending."

"I don't think so," Franklin declared. "We will win again."

"Yes," said Helen. "We will be victorious."

Connor laughed. "Never!"

As Connor laughed, Brett slammed his sword into him and splashed a potion, obliterating Connor.

"You destroyed him!" Helen screamed at Brett.

"How can we trap him if he's not here?" asked Kurt.

"I'm sorry. It was an accident." Brett nervously sipped a potion to regain his strength. "I was trying to make him weak and vulnerable. I wasn't trying to destroy him, but I guess I went too far."

Joe said, "It's okay. I hate the Nether, and I want to go back to the Overworld. He has respawned there, and we have to find him."

"Yes," said Helen. "Let's make a portal."

Franklin spotted something deeper in the cavern. "Guys, it looks like there's Nether quartz in here. I think we should mine for it."

"Not now." Helen was impatient. "We have to go find Connor."

"We will find Connor, but Nether quartz is very rare, and this might be one of our only opportunities to find it," said Joe.

Brett pulled his pickaxe from his inventory and banged it into the ground, unearthing Nether quartz.

He handed it to Joe. "You were right. It is here. You should put it in your inventory."

"This isn't the time," said Kurt. "I live in a cave, and I can tell you that most caves have treasures. I'm sure you'll find another one in the Nether at another point in time, and it will have a bunch of Nether quartz."

"That's not true." Joe was annoyed. "It's very hard to find. Brett, can you pick out some more?"

Franklin said, "You guys are wasting time. This isn't a trip to restock our inventories with resources from the Nether. We have a mission: we have to stop Connor. If we don't, we won't be able to save Meadow Mews. We have no idea how he is terrorizing the people of the town as we stand here in this cavern and discuss the benefits of mining for Nether quartz."

Everyone agreed they should craft a portal back to the Overworld. Even Joe didn't look back as they hurried from the cavern, which was teeming with Nether quartz. He had to be happy with the small portion that Brett had mined for him. As they came outside, they saw the sky filled with blazes, and they were forced to confront the yellow beasts with an arsenal of arrows and snowballs. The gang was down to a few hearts when they started to build the portal. As they hopped onto the portal, Brett sighed. He was happy to be out of the Nether, even though he knew they had a serious battle ahead of them.

When they emerged in the middle of the village in Meadow Mews, they were shocked to find the streets empty. The town was quiet, and it wasn't even filled with creepers.

"Where's everybody?" asked Helen.

Brett ducked into the blacksmith shop, but Lou the Blacksmith was missing. "Lou, are you here?" Brett called out, but there was no response.

Brett saw Helen coming out of the library, "Heather isn't in the either."

"Is anyone around?" asked Joe.

"We should knock on someone's door. We have to see if the townspeople are still in Meadow Mews. Maybe Connor was able to do something that got rid of all the villagers," suggested Nancy.

As Nancy spoke, a familiar face strolled down the eerily quiet main street. "Hey guys. What's up?" asked Bob, without a care in the world.

"Bob." Kurt ran toward him. "Where is everyone?"

"What?" Bob questioned. "Who are you talking about? Someone's missing?"

"We went into the shops, and all of the villagers are missing, but you're still here. How is that possible?" asked Helen.

"I had no idea that anybody was missing. I was just going back to the cave to look for you, but you weren't there. I was happy when I saw you walking through the village, Kurt," said Bob.

"We have to find the villagers," said Kurt.

"We also have to find out if anyone else is missing," said Nancy, "I'm going to knock on my friend Allie's door."

Helen looked up at the sky. The sun was setting. "Maybe we should go home and start searching for Connor and the others in the morning. I worry that we will be attacked by hostile mobs if we stay out now."

"Too late!" screamed Kurt.

As the sun began to set, a group of creepers silently entered the town. They detonated near the group, and Nancy was destroyed.

"Just try to make your way home," Franklin instructed them as they began to battle the creepers before the sun fully set and other hostile mobs spawned in Meadow Mews.

"What about me?" questioned Kurt. "Should I go back to the stronghold?"

"Come with us," said Brett. "We are staying with Nancy."

Kurt joined Brett and Joe as they shot arrows at the creepers and tried to race to Nancy's house. They narrowly avoided being destroyed as they made their way through the dusk.

As they hurried toward her house and away from the creepers, they heard a loud explosion in the distance.

Smoke rose, and Brett said, "Oh no! It looks like it's coming from Nancy's house."

14

FEELING GREEN

"**N**ancy!" Brett called out. She was standing in front of the rubble that was once her house.

"Are you okay?" asked Joe.

Nancy held a torch as she inspected the damage. "I'm fine. Thankfully, I wasn't in the house when it exploded."

"I bet the person who destroyed my tree house was the same person who blew up your house," said Brett.

"I'm sure it is," said Nancy as she watched four vacant-eyed zombies lumber toward them. "Guys, we have zombies."

"We have to find shelter," said Joe.

"It's too late to build anything," said Nancy. "Let's go to Helen's house. She doesn't live too far from here."

The zombies approached them with their arms extended. The smell from the rotten flesh made the gang gag, and they tried to hold their breath as they pierced the creatures of the night with their enchanted diamond swords. When they had slain the final zombie and picked up the dropped rotten flesh and placed it in their inventories, they raced toward Helen's house.

"Helen," Nancy said as she opened her door.

"Nancy!" Helen hollered. "Help me!"

Nancy stepped into Helen's house. "Where are you? What's wrong? We can help you!"

"Help!" Helen called out again, but this time her voice was lower and she was gasping for air.

Nancy, Joe, Kurt, and Brett raced through her house, opening every door as they called out for their friend Helen, but they couldn't find her. She had stopped calling for help, and the gang feared the worst.

Kurt said, "I think she's down here." He noticed a small hole in the corner of her house and climbed into it.

The hole led them to a long tunnel. Brett called out for Helen, but again there was no response. Brett pulled a torch from his inventory so he could see in the dimly lit tunnel.

"Ouch!" Nancy cried. She turned around and saw a bony skeleton behind her. She leaped toward the beast and attacked it with her diamond sword. The sound of clanging bones radiated through the small tunnel until she obliterated the skeleton.

"Help me!" Helen's voice was heard in the distance.

"She is down here!" Joe called out, and he raced toward the sound of Helen's voice.

"Helen," said Nancy, but there was no reply.

Joe opened a door and spotted Helen in a small dirt room. Connor was pointing a sword at Helen.

"I see you finally found your friend," Connor laughed.

"Why did you blow up my house?" asked Nancy.

"Why do you think I blew it up? Why would I do something like that?" he questioned with a snicker.

"Leave us alone!" Joe lunged at Connor, ripping into his shoulder with his enchanted diamond sword. "Stop attacking Meadow Mews."

"Why do you care so much about Meadow Mews?" asked Connor. "You don't even live here, Joe. Don't you live in Farmer's Bay?"

"I care about this town. My friends live here, and this was the first place that allowed me to create a large farm. It was one of the most exciting events of my life," said Joe.

"This town has lasted a lot longer than I ever expected. You're lucky that I didn't stage this attack earlier," he said as he slammed the sword on Helen's arm, leaving her with two hearts.

Helen cried out in pain, "Stop!"

"Why are you destroying Meadow Mews now?" asked Brett.

"I am going to leave the Overworld. Before I end my time here, I want to destroy Meadow Mews," he explained.

"That doesn't make sense," said Helen.

"It does to me," said Connor.

"You're just a griefer," said Joe. "People like you

never need reasons to cause trouble. You just want to destroy other people's happiness."

"That might be true, but I am being truthful. I am done with Minecraft, and I want to take Meadow Mews down before I go. I've already taken care of other things before I left, and this was the only one I had left. I have worked hard to rid the game of certain players."

"Are you talking about Poppy?" asked Brett.

"Poppy." Connor grinned. "I'm not sure."

"Tell me if you're behind her disappearance." Brett pointed his diamond sword at Connor.

"I'm not confessing to anything. I am just here to destroy Meadow Mews," said Connor.

"We will never let that happen," said Joe.

"Try and stop me," Connor said with a laugh, "and good luck getting out of here." With that comment, he splashed a potion of invisibility on himself and disappeared. The minute Connor was gone, creepers began to flood the tunnel.

"How are we going to get out of here?" asked Nancy. "If I get destroyed, where will I respawn? I don't even have a bed."

More creepers spawned in the narrow passage, and the gang was trapped. Brett fought the creepers with all of his energy. He had to find Connor. He knew he was hiding information about Poppy, and he'd battle a million green creepers in order to find his missing friend and to save the town he loved.

15

HIDDEN TREASURE

The creepers exploded, but the gang was able to avoid being destroyed by the silent but deadly mobs.

"I think I found a way out," Joe said. He banged his pickaxe against the wall of the tunnel as the others battled the creepers. He created a hole in the blocky wall and crawled through, away from the creepers into another room. The group followed him.

"This isn't a way out," cried Nancy. "We are trapped in this room"—she looked through the hole—"and that room is filling up with creepers. Soon they will be in here. We are trapped."

Brett suggested, "Why don't we TP out of here?"

"That is the simplest and most brilliant idea," Franklin remarked, and they TPed into the center of town. When they respawned in front of the blacksmith shop, it was still the middle of the night, and the gang found zombies ransacking the town. The undead beasts ripped doors from their hinges, looking for innocent villagers to transform into zombie villagers, but the town was empty.

"The villagers haven't returned," Helen remarked.

"Well, we can't go looking for them now." Franklin's voice cracked as he pointed to an army of skeletons that marched toward the small village. "We have to battle these skeletons."

"And the zombies," Nancy said breathlessly as she slammed her enchanted diamond sword into an awful-smelling zombie, destroying the beast with two strikes from her sword.

"Oh no!" cried Brett as he spotted creepers heading toward them. He didn't know if he should use a bow and arrow or a sword. "We have to get a strategy together, or we will never win this battle. I will battle the creepers. Who wants to join me? I think if we each focus on one mob, we won't be overwhelmed by all the mobs."

"I will battle the creepers with you," said Joe.

Brett was glad to have Joe by his side as they used their bows and arrows to annihilate this explosive mob.

Kurt and Nancy battled the zombies, and Helen and Franklin destroyed the skeletons. The battle went throughout the night. There were no breaks until the sun came up and offered them some relief from the battle. They looked at the sun with gratitude and exhaustion as they passed around potions and milk and any bits of food they had in their inventories to replenish their health.

"We have to find out where all of the villagers are being kept," said Helen.

"We have to find Connor," said Brett. "If we don't, we will never see an end to this. Also, I know he is behind Poppy's disappearance."

"I know you want to find Poppy," said Nancy, "but this isn't the time. We can't be sidetracked.

"I can't give up on her," Brett said.

They were all shocked when they heard a familiar voice say, "I'm afraid you're going to have to give up on her and also on the future of Meadow Mews." These words came from Connor's mouth. He stood in the center of the village and was joined by three people dressed in green suits with creeper heads.

"Who are they?" asked Brett as he aimed an arrow at one of them

"This is my army," Connor announced, "and there are many more soldiers ready to fight my battle."

Brett shot his arrow at the creeper-headed creature, destroying it. This angered Connor, and he charged toward Brett with a potion that he splashed on him. The potion weakened Brett. Connor whispered in Brett's ear, "I know where the portal is that will send you back to your time period."

Brett was weak and couldn't move. He barely had the strength to listen to Connor talk as Connor continued, "I am going to send you back to where you belong."

"How do you know I am from a different time period?" asked Brett. His voice was weak, and he struggled to speak those few words.

"I know everything," said Connor.

Franklin screamed, "What are you saying to Brett? Where are all the villagers?"

"It's none of your business what I'm saying to Brett, and the villagers are in a safe place. It wasn't right for me to let them stay here since I am destroying the town. If you guys were smart, you'd be like the other residents of Meadow Mews and you'd leave this town. Just let it end. Give it up," Connor lectured the group. "There are many functional towns that I have founded that you can relocate to. In fact, one of my greatest accomplishments is the creation of a wintery town called Hillsdale."

"Hillsdale?" cried Brett.

"Are you familiar with that town?" asked Connor.

"We built the farm for that town," said Joe.

"And I was building the farm when I—" Brett stopped talking. He didn't want to give Connor any more information about his situation.

Connor said, "I'm the person who created most of the towns in Minecraft, and because of that power, I also have the right to destroy them."

"No you don't," Helen said. "These are towns where people are living and enjoying their lives. You have no right to destroy them."

Brett wanted to go back to the past in order to save the future. If he could track down Connor in Hillsdale, he'd be able to avoid this confrontation in the future. He said, "Connor told me that he is going to make me leave you guys. I agree with him. I should leave this battle. It's not mine."

Helen, Franklin, Nancy, and Kurt were shocked. Even Bob, who strolled through the village and arrived to hear Brett speak, said, "What, you are abandoning everyone? That is not cool."

Brett wanted to let them know that he wasn't abandoning anyone. He was just trying to solve the problem before it even began, but he couldn't explain this and prove his dedication to his friends and the residents of Meadow Mews without giving up his plan. He was going to appear selfish when he was actually doing something that was selfless.

"I knew you were weak," said Connor with a smile. "Come with me." He held his enchanted diamond sword against Brett's back. "I am going to lead you to the portal. I don't trust you. You might change your mind, and we wouldn't want that to happen, right?"

"How can you do this?" Nancy asked. Brett looked at her blue eyes—they were somber and disappointed.

Brett didn't say anything as he walked out of Meadow Mews with Connor. The two people with creeper heads followed closely behind them. Brett could hear his friends gasp and caught snippets of comments: *How can he betray us? We thought he was our friend. We should never have trusted him.*

16

COLD STARES

Brett wasn't surprised when he saw his friends rush toward him. Connor called out, "You must stay in Meadow Mews. I am taking Brett back to his time period, and you aren't invited to come with us."

"You can't stop us," declared Helen.

"Yes, I can." Brett looked at his army of two and signaled them to attack. The two creeper-headed people leaped at the group with potions and their enchanted diamond swords. Nancy was the first to be destroyed, and Brett screamed. He wondered what would happen to Nancy. Her house was gone, and Brett wasn't sure where she'd respawn. He hoped this didn't mean that Nancy was gone forever. Tears streamed down his cheeks, but he was close to the portal, and he could feel the ice-cold breeze. His tears turned to icicles.

Connor said, "You better not have any last-minute

regrets. You made a good choice. You don't belong here. Your future self is gone and will never come back; I made sure of that, just like I did with Poppy."

The minute Brett heard Poppy's name, his heart began to race. Connor had just admitted that he was behind Poppy's disappearance, and Brett was furious.

"Where is Poppy?" Brett hollered. He tried to pull out his enchanted diamond sword. As he grabbed it, he thought he saw Poppy, her brown hair in braids and her signature purple jumpsuit on her body.

She called out, "Don't go, Brett. Stay here."

Brett tried to attack Connor and stay in Meadow Mews, but he didn't have a chance. Connor pushed him down the portal. As he fell deep into the hole, he could hear the sound of Poppy's voice in his ears while his body reacted to the frigid temperatures in the portal. Brett wanted to pull the black jacket he had worn when he was in Hillsdale from his inventory, but he was falling too quickly and wasn't capable of retrieving the warm jacket. His tears were frozen to his face, and his blond hair was frozen. He couldn't feel his feet or hands as he fell deeper into the portal, waiting to land, but it seemed as if this trip through the portal was a lot longer than the other ones he had taken. He took a deep breath and tried to relax as he waited to land in Hillsdale.

Splat! Brett landed on the icy ground of Hillsdale. He sprinted toward the farm. Joe was busy using his torch to melt the snow. "Isn't this exciting? I am so thrilled that we're able to build this farm."

Brett didn't even know where to begin. He wanted to tell Joe about falling down the portal and the future of Meadow Mews. He wanted to tell Joe that Connor was behind the creation of Hillsdale. He looked over at Poppy, Callie, and Laura working on the ice castle. Nobody was aware that he had fallen down the portal. It was just like the time he had arrived in the past with Joe. While he was away, the time hadn't registered. He looked at Joe and then he looked over at Poppy. Who would he tell first? And would they believe him?

He decided to confess to Joe what had happened. "I fell down a portal," he said. He felt that he should start with the basic facts first.

"What?" asked Joe. He was melting a large patch of snow, and the water was creating a puddle. "This is a lot more complex than we imagined. I don't think I have time for a story now."

"This isn't just a story. This is the future. Connor is the one who is creating Hillsdale," said Brett.

"What are you talking about?" Joe put the torch back in his inventory. Brett had captured his attention.

"I fell down a portal, like we did when we were working on the farm in Meadow Mews. This time, I fell down a portal and landed in the future."

"The future? Are we still friends in the future? Did you see me?" asked Joe.

"Yes," Brett replied and realized maybe he shouldn't have told Joe about his future, even if it was a positive fact. "But we shouldn't talk about our future. All I can say is that Meadow Mews is in trouble, and we have to save it."

"What's happening to Meadow Mews?" asked Joe.

"Connor has come back and is trying to destroy it," said Brett, "but if we stop him now, we might be able to help the people in the future."

"Where is Connor?" asked Joe.

Before Brett could answer Joe's question, Poppy called out, "Brett." She darted to him, her braids waving in the wind. Her purple jumpsuit was covered in a white down jacket. Callie and Laura followed behind her. They were talking about the ice castle.

Poppy said, "The castle is almost done. This is the fastest I have worked on a project. In all of my career I have never worked with people as great as Laura and Callie. I think we're going to work with one another for the rest of our careers, right?" She looked at her new friends and colleagues.

"Of course," they both replied eagerly as they chatted about the ice castle and the igloo and how it was the best work they had ever done.

Brett's eyes filled with tears. He wanted to tell them that they would work together for a long time and that one day they would be asked to create a building on Mushroom Island and they'd go missing. However, he knew they would be fine if he could just stop Connor now. If he could get their help to capture Connor and put him in prison, the future would be peaceful.

"You don't seem to be listening," Poppy said to Brett. She waved her hands in front of his eyes.

"Sorry," said Brett. "I was, but my mind is somewhere else."

"He just fell down a portal," explained Joe, "and he wound up in the future."

"Are we still friends in the future? Am I building great stuff with Callie and Laura?"

"It's funny, Joe asked if we were still friends, too," he said, and he tried to hide his emotions. He didn't want to tell her about the disappearance and how it shaped his future life. Brett said, "All I can tell you is that we have to find Connor. He is behind a large-scale attack in Meadow Mews."

"Isn't that the guy you battled in the past?" asked Poppy.

"Yes, and again in the future," replied Brett.

"How can we find him?" asked Poppy.

"Who is Connor?" asked Laura.

"It's a long story," said Joe, "but he's a total villain."

"How can we stop him?" questioned Callie.

"I have an idea," said Brett. "Follow me."

The gang followed him through the wintery terrain and toward the stage. They found the mayor standing with Harold the farmer. Harold was complaining about having to work with two inept farmers, and Brett's heart sank.

He had always loved Harold's work, and he couldn't believe Harold was dismissing his farming abilities. Brett couldn't let himself get distracted by this information. He had to focus, and he had to find Connor. He said, "Excuse me, mayor. I have to ask you a question."

"Can't you see I'm talking to him?" Harold was annoyed. "You shouldn't even be here. You're a weak farmer."

Joe defended Brett. "That isn't true. Brett is one of the best farmers in the Overworld."

"No, he isn't, and I can't believe someone like Connor would send both of you here. You're not up for the job," said Harold.

"Connor only handpicked the best talent in the Overworld. I don't think Brett and Joe are bad farmers," said Poppy.

"I'd like to talk to Connor," said Brett.

"If you want to tell him that you quit, I will lead you to him," Harold said with a smile.

"Where is he?" asked Joe.

"Connor doesn't want to be bothered," replied the mayor.

"It's very important that I speak to him," said Brett.

"I'm sorry, but I can't do that because I'm under orders to keep everyone away from him," explained the mayor.

"If we don't meet him, we will quit," Poppy threatened, "and we will also melt our ice castle."

"Connor remarked that the ice castle was the prettiest structure he had ever seen. Please don't do that," said the mayor.

"He saw the ice castle that we just finished? This means that he isn't far away," said Poppy. "If you don't tell us where he is, we will find him."

"Is that a threat?" questioned the mayor.

Poppy took out her enchanted diamond sword and pressed it against the mayor's unarmored chest. "Now it is."

17

WARRIORS

"**I** don't think this is a good idea," the mayor's voice cracked.

"Tell us where he is," demanded Poppy.

The gang followed the mayor through a snow-topped path until they reached a cave. "He's in here."

Brett and the group suited up in armor and grabbed their enchanted diamond swords from their inventory. Harold, who had followed the group, stood by the entrance to the cave. Brett asked him, "Why are you here? Why don't you go back to the farm and finish it? You don't want us there anyway, and now you can get a lot of work done without having to see us."

"I'm not going to miss this bit of entertainment. I am good friends with Connor, and I want to see him destroy you." Harold laughed. "You don't even deserve to be here. And I assume you're just as bad a fighter as you are a farmer."

Brett couldn't believe that he once idolized this farmer and wanted to ask him a series of questions about farming. It took all of his willpower not to strike Harold with his sword. He knew he had to save his energy for the battle against Connor.

Without saying a word to Harold, Brett and his friends walked into the cave. Brett didn't look back to see if Harold was following them. Poppy nearly slipped on an icy patch by the cave's entrance. But she steadied herself as she held on to a wall. Callie and Laura grabbed torches from their inventories. The ice on the ground melted from the warmth of the torches, and Brett's shoes filled with water and made a squishy sound as he walked.

"Your shoes are so loud," Poppy said to Brett.

"Yes, they are," a familiar voice called out. It was Connor. The light from the torch made him visible. Connor didn't have on any armor, but his beard had small icicles forming on it.

"How come you didn't tell us you were behind the creation of Hillsdale?" asked Brett.

"Would you have showed up?" asked Connor.

"Why would you invite us here, after everything that happened in the past, when we were founding Meadow Mews?" asked Joe.

"You guys are talented farmers." When Connor said this, Harold let out a loud laugh.

"So you did follow us in here, Harold," said Brett. He wanted to slam his sword into Harold, but he didn't.

"Yes," said Harold. "I told you I wanted to see what happens."

"Well, watch this." Brett walked up to Connor and pressed his sword against his chest. "I would never have accepted the invitation if I knew you were founding Hillsdale."

"Now you're here, and I must commend Poppy, Callie, and Laura for their incredible work on the ice castle. You have crafted a masterpiece in minutes. You didn't sacrifice any detail. I know that ice castle will be Hillsdale's main attraction, and people will travel from around the Overworld just to see it or stay in it. You are very talented, and I am going to make sure that I can have you work on all of my projects," said Connor.

Although Poppy despised Connor after hearing all of the stories Brett and Joe had told about him, she still blushed when he complimented her. She was proud of the ice castle, but she also wanted to destroy it. She was upset that she had created something so beautiful for Connor.

Brett knew that he must trap Connor. He pulled a potion from his inventory and splashed it on Connor. Despite being weakened from the potion, Connor had enough energy to pull his diamond sword from his inventory and strike Brett.

Joe leaped at Connor but didn't want to destroy him. They had to weaken him enough to trap him, which wasn't easy to do. Connor lunged at the group. He splashed potions on them and then shouted for the mayor.

The mayor had put on his armor and struck the group. Brett battled as he watched Poppy sprint away from the battle.

"Poppy," Brett called out.

"Looks like your best friend is abandoning you." Connor laughed as he slammed his sword into Brett's shoulder.

Brett was in pain. He wailed as he looked back for Poppy, but he couldn't see her.

He had two hearts left and didn't want to lose them. He struck Connor again and then jumped back. He pulled a potion from his inventory to regain his strength. As he took a break, he looked for Poppy and called her name again.

"I told you, Brett," Connor said, "she is gone."

"She'd never do that," Brett said as he swung his sword at Connor, but Connor was able to dodge the strike.

Brett didn't understand how Poppy could abandon him, but it all made sense when he heard her call out, "Brett! Over here!"

He turned around and saw a small bedrock structure that she had quickly crafted at the entrance to the cave. He had to get Connor into that makeshift prison.

18

SEE YOU SOON

"You think you're going to get me in there?" Connor laughed.

The mayor struck Laura with his diamond sword, destroying her. Callie screamed and lunged at the mayor, hitting him repeatedly until he vanished from the cold cave.

"You have nobody here to help you," said Brett as he and Joe cornered Connor.

"Harold!" Connor called out.

"I don't fight. You know that, Connor. I told you, I can't injure my hands. They are vital to me being a great farmer," Harold said and then excused himself. "There is nothing I can do to help you, so I am going to go back to the farm and create the best farm in the Overworld. I will make you proud."

"Proud? I don't want to be proud. I want to be free, and you have to help me," said Connor.

Harold didn't respond. He walked out of the cave without turning around.

Connor called out for the mayor, but Brett said, "He's gone too."

"He'll come back. He will TP here with an army and rescue me," declared Connor.

"If that's true, you can just wait for him in here," Joe said. He held his sword at Connor's back and led him into the bedrock prison with command blocks placed outside so Connor couldn't escape.

As they walked Connor into the small room, Laura called out, "Guys, do you need my help?"

"Yes," Callie said with a smile, "help us close Connor in here."

"You came back?" asked Connor. "But what about the mayor? Why didn't he return?"

"I saw the mayor. He was on stage announcing that he was the founder of Hillsdale and having a group of people create a plaque to note this important time in history."

This information infuriated Connor. "He's a traitor! Just like Grant was a traitor! I can't trust anyone!"

As they placed the final brick on the bedrock prison door, Brett walked over to the small window Poppy had carved out so they could feed Connor. Brett began to speak.

Connor pleaded, "I'm not in the mood to hear a lecture right now. Can you just leave me some food and let me be by myself for a bit?"

"I just wanted to tell you that your idea to create a town in the middle of the taiga was a great idea. I'm very excited to work on the farm, despite being berated by Harold. I also think you did a great job settling Farmer's Bay," said Brett.

Joe added, "And Farmer's Bay has been an incredible place to live."

"I am going to get your name added to the plaque as one of the founders of Hillsdale," Brett explained.

"But why?" Connor was stunned.

"You deserve the credit. I also want you to stop focusing on Meadow Mews," said Brett.

"How do you know what I think about Meadow Mews?" Connor was shocked.

"I know you're still upset that you weren't able to destroy it. I think you're a talented person who has great visions for settling new towns, and you shouldn't let your ego get in the way," said Brett. "If you stopped and realized how much you've done, you'd see what a special person you are."

Connor blushed. "I never thought of it that way."

"You'll have a lot of time to think about what you can do to change while you're in here. Hopefully, we won't have to keep you in here that long, and you can help us discover new places to develop. I think we can get a lot more done if we work together instead of fighting each other or trying to destroy places where people are living happily," said Brett.

Connor asked, "You guys would want to work with me?"

"Maybe," said Brett. "But we have to see you work toward changing."

"I'll try," said Connor.

Brett smiled. "I know you will. Now I'm going to create the best farm the taiga has ever seen, and I will come back to tell you about it."

"I look forward to hearing about it," said Connor.

As the gang left the cave and went back to work on developing Hillsdale, Brett smiled.

"What are you smiling about?" asked Poppy.

"I was just thinking about the future," replied Brett.

"I guess our future is going to be great," said Poppy.

Brett said, "Maybe, but I'm also excited about today. I can't wait to build the farm."

"You have to tour the ice castle," said Poppy.

"I just have one stop to make before we go to the ice castle," said Brett.

He walked toward the mayor, who was dictating what should be written on the plaque. Brett rushed over. "I just have one addition to the plaque."

The mayor looked annoyed. "What?"

"Please put Connor on the plaque. He also founded Hillsdale," said Brett.

The mayor was silent while the person who crafted the plaque added Connor's name. Brett smiled as he watched history being written.

The End